Dragon's Cave
Pirate Beach
Captain's Country
N

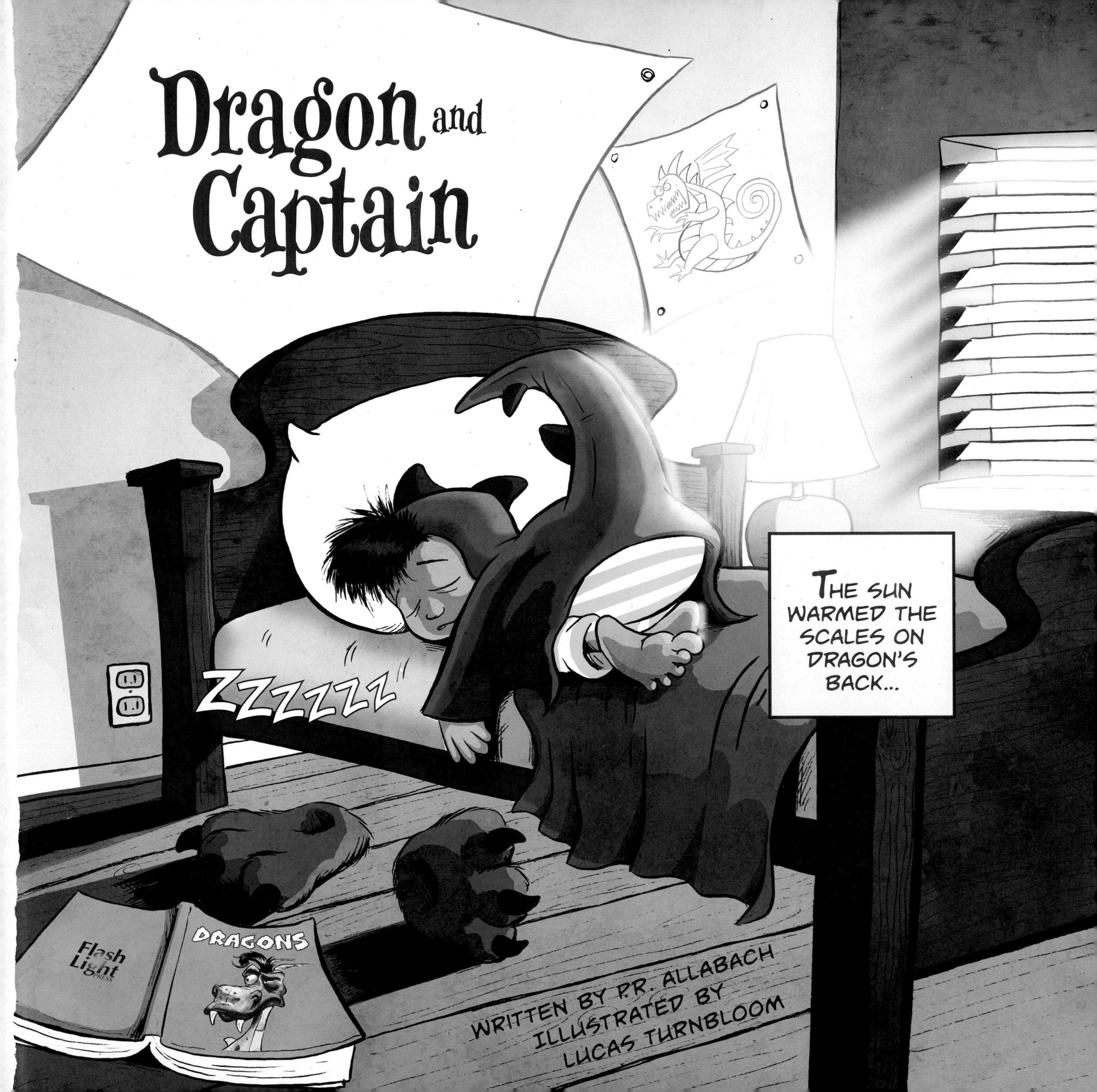
Dragon and Captain
THE SUN WARMED THE SCALES ON DRAGON'S BACK...
ZZZZZZ
DRAGONS
Flash Light PRESS
WRITTEN BY P.R. ALLABACH
ILLUSTRATED BY LUCAS TURNBLOOM

...AND THE SMELL OF OATMEAL FILLED HIS SNOUT. HIS STOMACH GROWLED.
HUNGRY.

FOR SARAH, LINDSEY, AND EMMETT,
I LOVE YOU! -PRA

TO ALEX AND AIDEN, MY OWN LITTLE
DRAGON AND CAPTAIN. -LT

PRINTED IN CHINA. ISBN 978-1-9362613-3-8

LIBRARY OF CONGRESS CONTROL NUMBER:
2014944932

EDITOR: SHARI DASH GREENSPAN
GRAPHIC DESIGN: THE VIRTUAL PAINTBRUSH

THIS BOOK IS TYPESET IN UNMASKED BB.
THE ART WAS CREATED USING GRAPHITE,
INKS, AND DIGITAL PAINT.

FLASHLIGHT PRESS
527 EMPIRE BLVD., BROOKLYN, NY 11225
WWW.FLASHLIGHTPRESS.COM

DISTRIBUTED BY IPG

munch
munch
THAT'S ODD. THERE'S A PIRATE IN MY SANDBOX. I MUST INVESTIGATE.
HEY, PIRATE. WHAT ARE YOU DOING IN MY SANDBOX?
I'M NOT A PIRATE, GOOD SIR. I'M THE CAPTAIN OF A SHIP.

DRAGON WENT OUTSIDE TO GET A CLOSER LOOK.
YOU *LOOK* LIKE A PIRATE. ARE YOU SURE YOU'RE NOT A PIRATE CAPTAIN?

I'M *NOT* A PIRATE CAPTAIN! I'M JUST A CAPTAIN!
AND, BY GEORGE, THERE'S NO TIME FOR QUESTIONS BECAUSE I'VE LOST MY SHIP.

OH, NO! I'LL HELP YOU FIND IT! COME ON!
WHERE ARE WE GOING?
TO MY CAVE!
LAND HO!
THOOMP THOOMP
THOOMP THOOMP

THOOMP
THOOMP
THOOMP
THOOMP

I **KNOW** I HAVE A MAP HERE SOMEWHERE.
FWOOP!

dragon's cave
captain's country
pirate beach
dark forest
craggy cliff
The Whole Sea
AH, HERE IT IS!
AND I FOUND A COMPASS AND A TELESCOPE!
PERFECT! JUST WHAT WE NEED.

NOW LOOK, CAPTAIN. TO FIND YOUR SHIP WE NEED TO GO THROUGH THIS FOREST, DOWN THIS CLIFF —
AND ALL THE WAY TO THE SEA!
DRAGON AND CAPTAIN RAN TO THE FOREST.
I WOULD FLY OVER THESE GIGANTIC TREES...

...BUT YOU DON'T HAVE WINGS SO WE'LL HAVE TO TREK THROUGH ON FOOT.

IT WAS A DIFFICULT JOURNEY...
MY WING!
MY HAT!
...AND IT GREW DARK AS THE THICK TREETOPS BLOCKED THE SUN.

DRAGON, I HEAR WATER! FOLLOW ME! FULL SPEED AHEAD!!
CAPTAIN PUSHED ON...

...BURST OUT OF THE FOREST...

AND STOPPED SHORT!
SKREEEEEEK!!

OOPS!

WHOA! WHERE DID THAT WATERFALL COME FROM?! I NEED TO FIX THIS MAP.

BLUBBERING BUBBLEGUM! I DON'T SEE MY SHIP! IT MUST BE LOST AT SEA.

DON'T WORRY, CAPTAIN. I'LL FIND IT FOR YOU.
DRAGON STEPPED TO THE EDGE OF THE CLIFF...
FLAPPED HIS MIGHTY WINGS...
...AND FLEW AROUND THE WHOLE SEA.
FLAP FLAP
FLAP FLAP

DID YOU FIND IT?
I THINK SO, CAPTAIN.

I FOUND TWO SHIPS! ONE HAS WHITE SAILS, BUT THE OTHER HAS BLACK SAILS — AND A *PIRATE* FLAG!
THUNDERING THUMBTACKS! EVIL PIRATES MUST HAVE CAPTURED MY SHIP.

WHAT SHOULD WE DO?
LET'S TRICK THEM AND PRETEND THAT WE'RE PIRATES.

HERE'S THE PLAN. WE'LL SNEAK PAST THE PIRATE GUARD AND BOARD MY SHIP. THEN ALL WE HAVE TO DO IS SAIL AWAY.
IT'S A PERFECT PLAN, CAPTAIN. THERE'S JUST ONE PROBLEM —

I DON'T LOOK ANYTHING LIKE A PIRATE!
HANG ON. I'VE GOT AN IDEA.

HERE. THESE CAN BE OUR HOOKS. NOW HAND ME THAT MAP.
CAPTAIN TURNED THE MAP.
HE FOLDED AND UNFOLDED
AND REFOLDED IT.
THEN CAPTAIN GAVE DRAGON THE BEST PIRATE HAT HE'D EVER SEEN.
FWUMP!

AARRRR! NOW DO I LOOK LIKE A PIRATE?
AYE, MATEY! BUT HIDE YOUR CLAWS AND TAIL.
hop
hop hop
SWISH!

CAPTAIN, YOU ARE A GENIUS.
NOW LET'S GET YOUR SHIP BACK FROM THOSE ROTTEN PIRATES!
DRAGON AND CAPTAIN SWAGGERED DOWN TO THE BEACH WHERE THE SHIPS WERE ANCHORED.

AHOY THERE, FELLOW PIRATE. WE'RE HERE TO, UMM, INSPECT THE ROPES ON THIS SHIP.

THE PIRATE GUARD STARED AT THEM BUT DIDN'T SAY A WORD.

THE PLAN IS WORKING! NOW LET'S GET OUT OF HERE! ANCHORS AWEIGH!

AND TO MAKE SURE THEY CAN'T FOLLOW US —
I'LL BLAST THEIR SHIP WITH FIRE!!

HURRAH!
ROAARR!!

WWHHSSHH!
WELL DONE, DRAGON! NOW FILL THE SAILS AND WE'LL HEAD FOR THE HIGH SEAS!
HUZZAH!

HUZZAH!
DRAGON AND CAPTAIN WATCHED THE PIRATE SHIP GROW SMALLER AS THEY SAILED AWAY.

SUDDENLY, A BREEZE MADE DRAGON'S SCALES STAND ON END. HIS STOMACH GROWLED.
HUNGRY.
YOU?
STARVING. WHY?
I SMELL MEATBALLS COMING FROM THAT CASTLE.
LET'S GO!!

HEY, CAPTAIN?
AYE, DRAGON?
IS YOUR SHIP FASTER THAN...
...A SEA MONSTER?!?

Unexplored!
dark forest
drag
Cav
Craggy Cli
The Whole